# A Visitation by Charles Dickens

*by Harrison Sheppard*

Cover Image: *Dickens' Dream* by Robert William Buss

Cover Design by Ariel Winnick

Aristotle & Alexander Press

191 Frederick Street, No. 23

San Francisco, CA 94117

**To Tom Woodhouse**
*fellow bibliophile and friend of English letters*


*The bones of this story have been largely plagiarized; but its flesh and skein are the author's own construction*

*"We meet on this day to celebrate the birthday of a vast army of living men and women who will live for ever with an actuality greater than that of the men and women whose external forms we see around us."* —Charles Dickens, at the Garrick Club, April 22, 1854, on the celebration of Shakespeare's birthday, as quoted by Christopher Hitchens in "The Dark Side of Dickens," *The Atlantic*, July 12, 2012.

*"I am ruminating,"* said Mr. Pickwick, *"on the strange mutability of human affairs."*

*"Ah, I see – in the palace door one day, out at the window the next. Philosopher, Sir?"*

*"An observer of human nature, sir,"* said Mr. Pickwick.

*"I would much rather have written Pickwick than to be Chief Justice of England, or a peer in Parliament."* —Attributed to John Campbell, Chief Justice and Lord High Chancellor of England (1779-1861), in John Forster: *The Life of Charles Dickens* (1874).

ii

# CONTENTS

1.  Five Characters     1

2.  Three Cups of Punch     6

3.  A Mystery is Explored by a Boy and A Young Man, and an Old Man Intervenes     9

4.  Three More Characters Appear to Help Raise A Tent     13

5.  Five Women Prepare for the Reception, and a Sixth Appears     19

6.  The Mystery is Further Explored by the Boy and the Young Man     22

7.  The Tent Is Raised And Floats Away To Sea     25

8.  The Boy and the Old Man Talk with Each Other About Youth and Old Age     30

9.  The Rescue of Two Characters, and Perhaps the Tent     33

10. Two New Friends and Two Old Friends Have Needed Conversations     38

11. The Young Man and His Beloved Converse Before the Fire     43

12. Preparation for the Reception Resumes     47

13. Charles Dickens Arrives and Is Questioned     49

14. Two New Lovers Meet     58

15. The Eldest Congregate and Consider Their Regard for Mr. Dickens     61

AFTERWORD & LITERARY NOTES     66

iv

# LIST OF CHARACTERS
## (IN ORDER OF APPEARANCE)

**JAMES STEERFORTH**, from *David Copperfield*, a privileged, utterly charming young man in his late twenties or early thirties, who shows a different character late in the novel

**SYDNEY CARTON**, from *A Tale of Two Cities*, a man approaching his forties, a drunk who ends up being a hero

**BETSEY TROTWOOD** ("Aunt Betsy"), from *David Copperfield*, David's loving but somewhat eccentric aunt, in her fifties

**MISS HAVISHAM**, from *Great Expectations*, a somewhat deranged woman in her sixties, who lives her life obsessed by memories of being jilted on her way to the altar, and who has raised her beautiful young ward, ESTELLA, to break the hearts of men

**PIP,** from *Great Expectations*, in his late twenties, ESTELLA'S long-time unrequited lover; a poor boy engaged by MISS HAVISHAM to amuse her who comes into good fortune and great expectations as the result of the generosity of an anonymous patron

**OLIVER TWIST**, from *Oliver Twist*, a destitute boy of about 14 (but shown beginning at nine years old in the book) who is kidnapped and forced to join a crew of underage criminals under the tutelage of a sinister man named Fagin (OLIVER'S story turns out well in the end)

**DAVID COPPERFIELD**, from *David Copperfield*, in his late twenties, (considered Dickens most autobiographical character), STEERFORTH'S younger, admiring boyhood friend, who becomes a successful writer

**EBENEZER SCROOGE,** from *A Christmas Carol*, about 70, a miser who has been reformed by the spirits of Christmas Past, Present, And Yet to Come and befriended the family of his put-upon employee, Bob Cratchit (father of Tiny Tim)

**WILKINS MICAWBER,** from *David Copperfield*, an impoverished man pushing 50 (played by W.C. Fields in the movie) with a large family, always expecting "something to turn up," who finds opportunity at the end of the novel in Australia; he befriends DAVID

**MAGWICH,** from *Great Expectations*, in his late 50's or early 60's, a one-time convict helped by the child PIP to escape and who makes his way to Australia, where he prospers and becomes the young man PIP'S anonymous benefactor

**GABRIEL GRUB,** from an obscure Dickens short story, "The Story of the Goblins Who Stole a Sexton," a church sexton and gravedigger about SCROOGE'S age, who prefigures Scrooge as a character through reformation of a nasty disposition as the result of an encounter with goblins

**PEGGOTTY,** from *David Copperfield*, in her 50's, DAVID's loving nurse in his happy early childhood who remains his friend after she is dismissed by his stepfather

**DORA COPPERFIELD**, from *David Copperfield*, in her twenties, DAVID'S airy-headed but lovable first wife (who dies young)

**AGNES WICKFIELD**, from *David Copperfield*, in her twenties, a portrait of the angelic but practical feminine, DAVID'S friend and later his second wife

**ESTELLA**, from *Great Expectations*, a few years older than PIP, raised as MISS HAVISHAM'S ward to "break men's hearts," hopelessly loved by PIP and discovered (late in the novel) to be MAGWICH'S natural daughter

**CHARLES DICKENS**, the author (1812-1870), appearing at about 50, after he had written all the works depicting the characters in this story

# A VISITATION BY CHARLES DICKENS

## by Harrison Sheppard

## 1. Five Characters

**The young man** remained as handsome, charming, jolly, gracious, and steadfast as ever, but at the moment he was scowling. He shook his curly blond head slowly in disbelief. "He's really coming to see us?" he asked, somewhat morosely.

"Why should that be so surprising?" replied his older companion, his eyebrows raised in skeptical wonder at the question, which he understood to be mainly rhetorical. "He was present at our creation; he's known us from birth. He is, after all, our father in a sense. And it's his 200th birthday!"

"I'm not sure I'm up to it," the younger lamented, "considering what he did to me. I'm not certain how I feel about him. He gave me a radiant glow of great promise, but for the sake of his drama did not permit me to realize it." He sniffed at recollection of the perceived injury done to him.

It was a February day, around noon, and they wore their greatcoats against the chill, made keener by stiff breezes coming off the sea. They were on the beach at Yarmouth, looking out at the swelling ocean. The rising northerly wind began to whip the water and sand into their faces. They turned away from the sea to take

1

shelter behind a large rowboat, tilted on its side and parallel to the incoming waves. The younger man sat down on the lip of its lowered edge. He placed an elbow on his knee and his square-jawed chin on his fist. The other man, named Sydney Carton, remained standing.

"Well," Carton answered in clipped cadences, "we both well know what the effects of drink and passion can do to a man. If it were not for your temperament, there was a far, far better thing you could have done with that lovely young girl. When all is said and done, were you not, after all, acting in the character he gave you? We've been told, have we not, that 'Character is fate.'?"

The junior gentleman, while remaining seated, protested vehemently. "There were good reasons young David—in fact, all my schoolmates—thought me their hero when I was introduced to readers. That was the character I should have remained to the end, despite my error with sweet Emily." He thought for another moment about the injustice he believed he had suffered. "Perhaps I should have a word with our author about the wrong done to me—if I stay to see him. What do you think?"

"I think, as he evidently did, that some of us begin life well but end it badly; others are fated to enjoy the reverse fortune."

"Yes," the still seated man returned, archly, "you were treated much more kindly by Mr. Dickens: *a hero in the end*. I was not that fortunate, but suffered instead the injustice of being painted a scoundrel with no excuse, despite my obvious virtues."

Carton considered continuing his side of the argument by asserting the consistency of the younger's character in both its admirable and feckless traits—

with the former degraded by snobbery. But before he could do so, the conversation was interrupted by the thwack of a closed umbrella on the prow of the boat.

"Get up from here at once!" demanded a black-clad elderly lady, accompanied by an even older, quite frail woman appearing in a white satin wedding dress, yellowed all about from long aging. "You villainous men," the second woman spat out caustically, "always inclined to evade your duty!" The umbrella-wielder, whose indignation was sharp but milder than her companion's, took a softer but still demanding tone: "You're needed, gentlemen, to help us with arrangements for the reception, up yonder at the Peggottys' house." She reinforced her demand by adding, in her own harshest tone: "Terminate your lollygagging and come with us at once!"

James Steerforth rose from his makeshift seat and gave a respectful bow. "Of course, Miss Trotwood; we'll be glad to help." First glancing at Carton with a concealed wink, he returned his gaze to the women. He chivalrously asked, "How may we be of assistance, dear ladies?" With the utmost skill and the utmost ease, he set about to pacify their mood. He moved forward gracefully on the unsoaked sand and placed himself between Betsey Trotwood and Miss Havisham. Extending his elbows, he wordlessly invited them to take his arms in theirs for the walk up to the Peggottys' home. They were charmed, for the moment, out of their indignation and accepted the invitation, each shyly linking an arm with his. "Carton," Steerforth pleaded courteously without looking back, "please do join us." Carton, correctly perceiving which of the two would be most grateful for a second friendly arm, aligned himself with the three at the side of Miss Havisham. The

3

foursome moved slowly together toward the house, the wind at their backs, as Steerforth chatted up Miss Trotwood. "Will Mr. Dick be joining us?" he inquired with solicitude.

"Mr. Dick ain't coming," Miss Trotwood answered. "In his unfailing wisdom, he observed that the Peggottys would need a circus tent to accommodate the crowd that will be likely to gather to meet Mr. Dickens. And that is the very reason, Mr. Steerforth, we need your help and your friend's—to put up a tent. The Peggottys' house is not a very large one, as I'm sure you know quite well. As for Mr. Dick's declining to join us, he gave the additional reason that since Mr. Dickens already knows everything in Mr. Dick's head, there was no use in his being here to bother him with whatever he might say on meeting him—or not say, for that matter."

"Do you suppose, Miss Trotwood," Steerforth asked casually, disguising the depth of his interest in the question, "that any of us could actually say anything that would bother Mr. Dickens?"

"I make no such suppositions, young man. You must decide that for yourself. I will point out, however, that Mr. Dickens is a man of very refined sensibilities and therefore doubtlessly not immune to the sentiments of others as regards himself."

As they neared the Peggottys' house on their upward climb, still aided by the push of the wind, they watched a tall young man moving toward them in long strides, not exactly running, but clearly exhibiting an eagerness to meet up with them. By the time the lad came near enough to be recognized and easily heard, it was apparent that the main object of his interest was an encounter with Miss Havisham. In his eagerness for the reunion, without greeting the others, he addressed her

4

directly. "Miss Havisham," he enthused, "it's really lovely to see you again. Lovely. But I see Estella is not with you." And then he asked, in a decidedly diffident tone, "May we expect her before Mr. Dickens arrives?"

"Ah, still hopelessly in love, I am pleased to see. Whether Estella joins the party will be up to her. I really can't say whether your being here will discourage or encourage her presence. I rather think the latter. But you should not depend upon my opinion of the matter. Estella has very much a mind of her own now. And as interested as I am to know how *you* are, Pip, I'm afraid we both have forgot our manners. May I introduce you to my friends?"

Separated from each other by Pip's exchange with Miss Havisham, her three companions remained standing beside her, politely attentive. "Oh," Pip offered, "I have met Mr. Steerforth in London, but I am unacquainted with the other gentleman and the lady." Introductions were properly made and polite salutations exchanged all round among the newly acquainted—including Carton and Trotwood. The five of them then walked ensemble up to the house, the original four completing their journey in more convivial moods than the ones in which they had started out. (Pip, however, omitted to give an account of himself to Miss Havisham.)

# 2. Three Cups of Punch

The quintet arrived at the Peggottys' house, entering at the front door, which opened directly into the sparsely furnished sitting room. A large upholstered chair, usually accommodating the master of the house, with a little wood table beside it, and a rocking chair, composed its main furniture. In addition, a number of smaller chairs were scattered about the wooden floor. The room's only other accoutrement, apart from the fireplace equipage, was a woven rug, three or four feet square, placed in its middle, modestly adding to the room's homeyness. On their entry, Miss Trotwood addressed Steerforth and Carton: "Kindly come with me into the kitchen. The canvas for the tent is lying behind the house, and you can get to it through the kitchen. Pip can show you the way; he's already been helping prepare for the raising of the tent. There's a warm bowl of punch on the kitchen table. I shall have no objection if you choose to refresh and arm yourself against the cold with a cup of it on your way through."

The three men followed Miss Trotwood into the kitchen and cheerfully accepted her invitation to the punchbowl. As they sipped their drinks, Steerforth asked: "Pray remind me, Mr. Pip, where was it that I had the pleasure of meeting you in London?"

"I recall it well, Mr. Steerforth. It was at the tavern nearest the Old Bailey. I had been visiting my solicitor, Mr. Jaggers, who had been in court, and the two of us stopped at the tavern nearby for a glass or two of port. That was where we met. I believe you had had

6

some business with a solicitor who had rooms at the same Inn as Mr. Jaggers, and he introduced us."

"That tavern was still there, eh?" Carton inquired with nostalgia. "I spent many an hour at that tavern, and well into the night, I should tell you."

"It was a rare visit for me, Mr. Carton," Steerforth commented. "My usual habit," he sniffed, "is to enjoy my drink in more commodious settings, in proximity to more inviting environs than the Old Bailey." He turned his attention back to Pip. "Our meeting was a brief one then, I suppose?"

"It was indeed. You excused yourself rather quickly, at a reminder by your man—Littimer was his name, as I recall—that you had another engagement to attend."

"I gather then, Steerforth," Carton continued his part of the conversation, annoyed at Steerforth's implicit boast of greater discrimination, "that you don't find the pleasure of good drink in the company of a convivial crowd of like-minded gentlemen a sufficient inducement to your participation in tavern life."

"You can never be sure, with a tavern, Mr. Carton, that the so-called 'gentlemen' you encounter are either like-minded or like situated, and I don't enjoy *scenes*," Steerforth retorted. He went on: "Mr. Pip was congenial enough, as I now recall, but I doubt—excuse me for saying so, Pip—that our both residing in London would alone give much ground for supposing that we would have many interests or associations in common; although, to be fair, despite his evident new arrival in the city, I did take him for a gentleman."

Notwithstanding the attempted mitigation of condescension in Steerforth's remarks, they could not help but embarrass Pip. Sensitive to Pip's discomfort,

Carton diverted the conversation by reminding Steerforth of their promise to assist with the tent forthwith. Steerforth took the hint, and the two prepared to make their exit. "Won't you excuse us, old chap?," Carton pleaded to Pip. "I look forward with pleasure to extending our acquaintance, perhaps with another cup," he said, giving Pip a convivial tap on the shoulder as he departed.

Pip remained in the kitchen, still slowly sipping his cup of punch.

## 3. A Mystery is Explored by a Boy and A Young Man, and an Old Man Intervenes

"What I want to know, Mr. Copperfield, if you'd be good enough to tell me, is: how is it possible for all of us to meet Mr. Dickens if some of us is *dead*, according to the stories of his books?" David, more nearly Dickens' avatar than any other one of his characters, placed a kindly hand on the boy's shoulder, and smiled at the question. They were standing in the sitting room, warming themselves before the fire lighted against the icy winds chilling the house.

"Well, Twist, why don't we sit down and I'll try to explain it to you as best I can." They took chairs on opposite sides of the fireplace and moved them inward toward each other. Oliver was eager to learn the answer to his question and, after bringing his chair even closer to David's, leaned forward to hear it.

Copperfield searched for words to begin his reply. His eyes moved upwards toward the ceiling. "Let's see. I agree it is difficult to understand. Quite perplexing in fact." Having gathered his thoughts, he fastened his eyes on those of the attentive boy. "The answer will no doubt surprise you, Twist. We characters might rightly say that it is less credible that Mr. Dickens should come to visit us than it is that we'd be here to receive him. What do you think of that?"

The boy wrinkled his brow and squinched his nose. "How is that, sir? You must give more of an

9

explanation than that, if you don't mind my saying so, if I am to understand it. Please, sir, I do want to know more."

"Quite right," acknowledged the elder, fully aware that his reply to the question was a mere tease, not really an answer. "Well, Oliver, it's the *characters* created by an author who become immortal. It is their author, not them, who passes through a limited number of days on earth. Think of it. Here it is, 200 years after Mr. Dickens was born, and you and I and my Aunt Betsy and all the rest of us still inhabit the same space we always did: in his books. We remain ready to be seen and heard and thought about by anyone who chooses to pick up the book in which we appear; and we continue to live out our lives, *immortally*. Fiction, in other words, one might say, *may be* stranger—and more enduring—than fact or mundane truth. Depending, of course, on what you mean by 'truth.' Some maintain that the greatest works of fiction resonate with far more truth than what we will find in a newspaper. And we fictional beings always remain true to who we are from the time we are created and presented to the world."

Oliver, ever quick in understanding, slapped his little hand upon his forehead. "Of course, Mr. Copperfield!" he virtually shouted. "I should've been able to think of that myself. I'm very much over a hundred years old, but look at me. *I'm still just a boy.* I suppose what you said explains *that.*"

Now it was Oliver who looked upward in an effort to collect his thoughts. He had a new question on the tip of his tongue. "But then," he began his fresh inquiry, looking down from the ceiling to meet Copperfield's eyes, "as what you have said makes ever

10

so clear, there's the puzzling question of *Mr. Dickens* showing up. He really is dead, ain't he?"

"Bah, humbug!" an agitated voice was heard in apparent protest. "I once thought any idea about the eternal was humbug." These equivocal declarations came from an old man theretofore standing in silence at the lone windowpane glass on the opposite side of the room from the fireplace. Having overheard the conversation between David and Oliver, the man was moved by David's remarks to offer his perspective on the inquiry. Walking to the side of the chair on which Oliver sat, he looked down upon the boy with tears in his eyes and a lump in his throat. Clearing his throat, he prepared himself to remove the ambiguity of his assertions. "But I have emphatically thought some other very sound sayings were humbug and learned to repent my mistaken certainty." He addressed Oliver in a gentle, in fact, in an affectionate tone. "You are a clever boy. A clever boy indeed. But you must, I advise you"—he turned to include David in his advice—"we all must, in point of fact, leave it to Mr. Dickens to explain his appearance when he arrives."

The old gentleman pulled a large white handkerchief out of his pocket and wiped away his nascent tears. His face transformed from its look of saddened nostalgia into the happy curve of a smile. He continued to address both David and Oliver: "But for now, while we await the arrival of our author, I invite each of you to enjoy a cup of punch with me, from a deliciously warm bowl of it whose whereabouts I happen to know." The seated pair, stunned to silence by both the interjection and the invitation, rose from their chairs. Each gave a polite nod to the old man. Ebenezer Scrooge took Oliver's hand in his and marched him, with

David following, toward the warm bowl of sweet punch sitting on the table in the kitchen. "You'll want more after your first cup of it, my boy," he warned Oliver, "but not too much more."

# 4. Three More Characters Appear to Help Raise A Tent

The immense canvas tent Betsey Trotwood brought—with a great deal of difficulty I should tell you—to accommodate the reception crowd lay wrinkled where it had been thrown upon the ground behind the Peggottys' house.  Two men were in the process of trying to smooth it out when Steerforth and Carton joined them.  Perceiving no particular plan in the efforts the two workmen were making, Steerforth took immediate charge of the project.  "Micawber," he shouted out from a distance with a tincture of sarcasm, "who is that fellow on the other side of the canvas doing as much as you are to get this job properly done?"

Wilkins Micawber's back was to Steerforth but, to those who knew him, his identity was evident from his rotund, pear-shaped figure. He raised his head, all but engulfed by the muffler around his neck shielding him from the cold. Ceasing his struggles with the canvas, he turned to face his inquisitor, whom he also recognized at once. "Hallo, my dear boy," he replied in greeting, "how good of you to turn up to give us a helping hand!  In fact, I conceive, if I am not in error, that you have brought *four* hands to facilitate the navigation of this stupendous amplitude of praetorium into a commodious form of habitation.  Completion of the task will, I venture to say, either take all the nimbleness of a practiced prestidigitator or a multitudinous consortium of laborers.  It may be, however, that although a greater number would be

13

more optimum, we will not deceive ourselves if we entertain the hope that the eight hands we possess among us will be adequate to compose such an assemblage.

"But I have digressed in my greeting from the import of your interrogatory. The good man on the far side of this formidable shelter-to-be calls himself Magwich." Magwich, hearing his name pronounced, looked up from his work. He raised himself to his full height, which was made to seem all the greater by the sturdy bulk of his frame. His bald head seemed to pop out from inside his large ears, and his unshaven scraggly face gave him a dangerous look. He nodded in salutation to the newcomers. Acknowledging Magwich's person further, Micawber continued his introduction of the man. "We have only just this morning had the pleasure of making each other's acquaintance. I have discovered we share a common interest in the prospects available to the enterprising in the land down under, prospects Magwich has explored with quite extraordinary success."

"All to the good, Micawber," Steerforth replied with curt encouragement, returning a polite nod to Magwich. "Now where are the stakes we must have to organize the tent?"

Before Micawber could venture a circumlocutous, sesquipedeliant reply to a question he could not have answered, another grizzled old man, his lanky frame slightly bent with the weight of the load he was bringing to the work party, shuffled himself between Micawber and Steerforth. "They are right here, in this sack I'm carryin'." The stranger raised a large canvas sack as high as he could to facilitate its visibility to the men dispersed at opposing points about the splayed tent. He dropped the sack upon the ground and headed directly toward Steerforth, whose emerging dominance of the scene had been immediately apparent to him as he approached it. Offering a dirty, wrinkled hand to Steerforth, he introduced himself: "Gabriel Grub is who I am. To whom do I have the honor of addressin'?" Steerforth restrained an impulse to recoil from Grub's grimy-handed offer. He responded to it with a barely courteous nod in reply, made a little more polite with his saying, "James Steerforth, at your service."

"You're not sure you like the looks of me, eh, young fellow?" queried Grub. "If you have the acquaintance of Ebenezer Scrooge, he can tell ya I'm not quite what I appear to be, though I once was, when I served as a sexton in an abbey town quite a bit away from here. But I'm free of those cares now. *The goblins'll getch ya if you don't watch out!*" Grub uttered these last words with a wide, toothless smile, and punctuated them with a lightfooted skip and an outright laugh. Steerforth took him to be a little mad and, ignoring the man's rude question, resumed his position of command. "Magwich, my good man," he shouted, "kindly come join us. It would be best if we gather round and plan our method of attack on this thing." In response to this tactical admonition, the three older men were pleased to assemble themselves close to Steerforth. Carton remained nearby, but stood in silence outside the rough square formed by the gentleman and his recruits. He was not wholly indifferent to what they were about, but wished to keep an independent perspective on how things might progress.

Grub's mention of Scrooge was nearly synchronous with the coming event. Steerforth, having surveyed the entire scene surrounding the canvas, began to share with the others his thinking about the best procedure for raising the tent. Before he had gone on very long, Scrooge, Pip, and Copperfield emerged from the rear of the house. Their punch cups quaffed and no longer in hand, with jolly spirits—Pip having joined the other two for another helping of punch to ease both his embarrassment and his anxious anticipation of Estella's arrival—they had become curious about the status of the work they knew to be in progress. Despite the ubiquitous noise of a continually howling northerly wind, the approaching steps of the three on the hardened ground were quite audible. Steerforth turned toward the sound to ascertain what it signified.

Nearing the work party, Scrooge spied old Grub and Pip spotted Magwich, with whom he had already worked that morning on preparations for the tent. They left Copperfield's side to join their respective former mentors. Simultaneously, Steerforth recognized David. At the sight of him, Steerforth's aplomb vanished. He blushed, and hesitated to continue laying out his work plan to the others.

Copperfield was likewise perturbed by seeing Steerforth at the Peggotty's home. But his older school chum, a man almost never at a loss, instantly grasped the need to put David at his ease. He speedily willed himself to recover from his own embarrassment. Breaking from the workman group, he approached his long-time friend with a steady gait. Addressing him by the nickname he had given him in their school days, and observing the fine figure Copperfield made in his own elegant greatcoat, Steerforth greeted David with warmth. "My, Daisy," he exclaimed, "how you do prosper!"

"Thank you, Steerforth," Copperfield replied, quietly. Then, in a tone more of sorrow than of anger: "I'm surprised to see you here, of all places." Steerforth, now within arm's reach of David, lowered his voice as well, almost to a whisper. "I'm certain that not all that happened has been rightly explained to you," he first said. "I wish with all my soul I had been better guided and could have guided myself better. But if I was not entirely innocent, I was never so wanton or wicked as it might have seemed." He clasped David by the shoulder. "I have never lost my feelings of affection for you, David, or trust in your goodness. We owe it to the love we bear each other to reach a better understanding. We must talk. And you must, as I asked you before I left with Emily, think of me at my best."

"I always have, Steerforth; I still do, and I always will."

When it came to an object he had determined to achieve, Steerforth's willfulness, and the power of his charm, of which he was keenly aware, had at times a tendency to overtake his good judgment and his sense of propriety. The slender dam of his self-restraint was easily burst, and the slim pillars of his moral virtues were readily bent, by any flood of his emotion, especially when provoked by indignation, an object of strong affection, or an assault upon his dignity. His embarrasment at David's appearance might have seemed to him to have been incited by one or more such provocations. In any case, it was certainly one of his objects to retain the good opinion of his greatest schoolboy chum, whom he did truly love. Whether it was mainly his love or, rather, his intemperate willfulness that was the foundation of his appeal to David for greater understanding had yet to be seen. It was not the proper moment or setting, however, for the conversation he wished to have with David. But Steerforth had determined for himself that the right moment would come. In the mean time, he turned David's attention to the task at hand, requesting his assistance in the project.

Steerforth having left the group, and Carton guessing rightly at the cause of the incoming trio's jollity, the latter excused himself from the scene and returned to the house. His purpose was to warm and gratify himself with another cup of punch from the bowl sitting on the kitchen table. (Enjoying *flagons* of punch was one of his favorite pastimes.) On his arrival in the kitchen, in the midst of the members of the opposite sex gathered there, he was able to pacify his usual discomfort with the society of women by swiftly imbibing two overfull cups of punch, immediately exiting thereafter to see what further assistance his refreshment might enable him to render to Steerforth.

# 5. Five Women Prepare for the Reception, and a Sixth Appears

Betsey Trotwood had taken the same command inside the house that Steerforth ventured to exercise outside of it. In the absence of servants, she was organizing the efforts of four other ladies already present for the reception, all but one of whom was accustomed to having others do such work for them. These consisted of Miss Havisham; Peggotty (the mistress of the house, quite familiar with the arts and labors of the kitchen); and Dora Copperfield and Agnes Wickfield (David's wife, and friend and future wife, respectively). They were all busy preparing the comestibles for the celebration of Mr. Dickens' arrival.

Oliver, warmed by the cup of punch Scrooge had poured for him before going out to visit with the other men, and pampered by both Peggotty and Agnes, looked happily on from a side chair in the crowded kitchen, a dish of biscuits placed within his reach. "Shall we have a cake?" he innocently asked, thinking he was directing his question to Miss Trotwood. That lady was, however, busily engaged, and failed to hear it. Miss Havisham was irritated by the inquiry, having in mind an uneaten wedding cake of which she was always conscious. She replied to Oliver testily: "There will be a *birthday* cake, boy. A birthday cake, just now baking in the oven."

"And a fine beefsteak pie, too," added Peggotty, more cheerfully.

"What is this about cakes and pies?" inquired Aunt Betsey, her awareness returned. "The boy was asking about cake," replied Miss Havisham, "and I informed him of the kind of cake we will have."

"And what is more natural, Miss Havisham, than that a boy should ask about cake?" Aunt Betsey declared. "Stop your brooding and put your mind and hands to use. Come help me, if you please."

In addition to Peggotty's baked delectables, and the enormous quantity of punch that had been concocted, there was a variety of store-bought foods purchased for the celebration. These included new loaves of bread and fresh biscuits; cheeses and bacon; a side of lamb; butter, honey, mint sauce, and walnut ketchup; and tea and coffee, all of which needed to be properly prepared and arranged for their presentation and enjoyment. While the ladies were busily engaged in doing so, David Copperfield appeared at the kitchen door, passing Carton on the way out. He was on an errand at Steerforth's request whose necessity had come as a welcome relief from the disquieting scene that had passed between them.

"Trot," Aunt Betsey addressed her nephew, "there's no need for you here at the moment. The kitchen is already too full. Are you not engaged with the other gentlemen in raising the tent?" "Indeed, Aunt Betsey," he replied. "I am here only to ask Peggotty where we may find some hammers or mallets to put in the stakes."

"I wonder," Peggotty replied with glowing affection, "that you do not recall where Mr. Peggotty's chest of tools is located. It is where it always has been."

"*Of course,*" David answered with chagrin. "I, I, I must have lost my wits," he stuttered. "It had just gone out of my mind. I'm afraid something distracted me." He moved toward the doorway from which he had

20

entered but once again met with contrary traffic as he encountered Estella just arriving at the portal. He made way for her before he exited. She, with the same enthusiasm Pip had shown in spotting Miss Havisham, likewise went directly to that venerable lady without a word to anyone else. "Well, you *have* decided to come, Estella," Miss Havisham remarked to her former ward, with no other greeting. "You must know that Pip is here. He has already asked after you, and I think you should make a point to visit with him when he has finished with the work he is about outside the house."

"If it should break his heart not to see me, then I shall let him make a point to visit *me*," Estella replied, in a proud tone colder than the wind blowing outside the house, into its cracks, and through its openings.

With these distractions from the interesting kitchen doings of the women, Oliver slid off his chair and followed David. He had another question for Copperfield about the reception for Mr. Dickens. The boy reached his pre-occupied literary tutor just before he was able to exit the door to fetch the tools whose obtaining had been his accepted errand.

## 6. The Mystery is Further Explored by the Boy and the Young Man

The boy, upon obtaining his tutor's attention, began his inquiry. "Mr. Copperfield, sir," I have another question for you. May we sit for a moment again by the fire?"

"I really must return to our work on the tent, Twist," David replied, distractedly. "But what is it? What would you like to know? I'll answer if I can. But pray be brief about it."

"Will we *all* be here? I mean, will I have to see Mr. Fagin and all his boys again? That would not be very pleasant, I can tell you." The keenness of David's empathy for the boy on hearing his poignant question enabled Copperfield to let go of his troubled state of mind. "Well," he said, "a few more moments shouldn't raise any difficulties, Oliver. Of course we can sit by the fire for a bit while we ponder your question."

He led the boy toward the seat he had taken by the fireplace before Scrooge's interruption of their conversation, and then likewise re-seated himself. Their faces again close to each other's, they regarded one another in silence for a few moments. David put the fingertips of both his hands together and raised them to his chin as he looked with sympathy at the attentive boy. He took a deep breath. "I do not credit the possibility," he said after his pause for thought and preparation for speech, "that we will *all* be here. Notwithstanding the large tent we are raising, if all of Mr. Dickens' characters were to attend, they would compose far too numerous a crowd to give him—or them—any particular pleasure in his visit. And I would suggest that your very presence here, Oliver, considering Mr. Dickens' great fondness for you, foretells the probability that neither Fagin nor his boys will be among the guests gathered here for his reception. I can make no *promise* about that, to be sure, but that is my earnest conjecture."

He paused for thought once again, in an effort to anticipate what Oliver might ask next, and then correctly foresaw the boy's consequent question, even though it had not yet been spoken. "My conjecture may not, however, embody a *principle of selection*. As to discovering the factors deciding who will be in attendance and who will not, we must either allow our observations and logical inferences to be our guides, or inquire of Mr. Dickens himself when he arrives whom *he* would choose to admit to his company on this occasion."

Copperfield took another deep breath, waiting to see if the boy had absorbed what he had been told. Oliver was gingerly bobbing his head up and down, permitting Copperfield to infer that he had grasped the substance of the answer given to him, and its qualifications. But Charles Dickens' most autobiographical character had not yet completed what he wished to say to Oliver Twist. He resumed the tutorial: "There is another, not unrelated question, Oliver, to which we will need to give some thought. And that is this: What can we say to account for the choice of the time of events or age at which our literary brothers and sisters will make their appearance on this occasion? The whole of their being remains fixed and forever in existence. But what of them shall manifest today, and why?" He punctuated this question with a decisive silence, prefacing his departure.

"I must now leave you, Mr. Twist, so you may ponder the question, while I attend to my duty to help raise the tent." With this affirmation of his departure and indication of the end of his instruction, Copperfield rose from his chair, leaving Oliver sitting in front of the fire to contemplate the provocative issue that had been raised about the guest list.

# 7. The Tent Is Raised And Floats Away To Sea

Scrooge had no taste for the outdoors on a cold, windy day, separated from the warmth of a fireplace and bowl of punch, the latter of which Carton had just twice enjoyed before reappearing. After a brief but cordial conversation with Grub, Scrooge returned to the comforts of the house to allow the hardier men to continue to do the work that had to be done. Steerforth, having made a transition with Copperfield from their private conversation to a request for his assistance in tool-gathering, resumed his command. Soon all those remaining outside the house were working at their respective assignments under the joint surveillance of Steerforth and Carton, while awaiting Copperfield's return with the tools needed to plant the stakes.

It was Steerforth who, in consultation with Carton, devised the overall plan and allotted particular tasks to his aged crew. But it was Magwich and Micawber who together calculated the arrangement of the splayed canvas that would best accommodate the stakes and centerpole and allow the finished tent to be raised to its proper height. Grub, whose gravedigging duties as a sexton had prepared him well for the task of breaking hardened ground, was swiftly completing the job, circumnavigating the canvas with a pick and following the markers Magwich had made for placement of the stakes.

Copperfield returned to the scene of work with two hammers and two mallets in his hands, having searched out and found them in the Peggotty tool chest. "Ah, thank you, David;" Steerforth said in renewed greeting, "of course you were the right man for the job." And then he added: "Micawber, Magwich, and the sexton are, I think, ready for those. And I pray you will use the fourth implement to give those old chaps some help." Copperfield distributed the tools as directed, keeping a mallet for himself, and the planting of the stakes was begun.

It soon became apparent that Magwich was the champion of the endeavor. His powerful arms brought his hammer down upon each stake he worked with such force, that in only one or two strokes it sunk into the hard ground as far as it could go and still be of use to anchor the tent. Witnessing this phenomenon, the others were so impressed they stopped their own work. "My good sir," Micawber called to Magwich, "how would it strike you if we leave it to you to hammer *all* the stakes down as you are doing, all round the tent?" Magwich looked up and around to his fellows with a proud smile. "It'd be me privilege to do so," he declaimed. "There ain't but a score or so of 'em to get the job done right and complete." Steerforth approved. He then politely requested Grub and Pip, who were nearest to its position on the ground, to bring the centerpole round to the side where the tent flaps would be opened.

A winch had earlier been arranged by Magwich and Pip to raise the tent. Grub's efficiency, and Magwich's, had combined to bring the moment when the tent was ready to be raised. The continual northerly winds were a complicating, bothersome factor. It required some care—and, as it proved—repeatedly frustrated efforts to raise the tent while it suffered repeated dislocations from the wind whipping and rippling the canvas. After ordering Grub to tie the tent top soundly to the winch line, Steerforth volunteered himself and Carton to operate the apparatus, which he conceived as the most crucial part of the project. The two gentlemen undertook this labor with great energy. But, as soon as the canvas had reached a height where the flaps of the tent could be opened to form a portal, the real trouble began.

The wind had been rising all afternoon. Just at the wrong moment, it turned into a squall. The stakes had been laid, and the canvas attached to them securely; but not, as it turned out, quite securely enough. The tent rippled in the wind with such force, that some of its ties became loosened. A tremendous burst of air, in a broad spear of intense pressure, entered the tent and began to billow it, then expand it to its full capacity. Magwich, Micawber, Pip, and Grub, fighting valiantly with the wind, all struggled with the lines to the stakes as the squall continued to increase in fury. Then, in a great burst of nearly hurricane force, the gales of air ripped the canvas entirely loose from its moorings and it began to sail upward, remaining attached to the ground only by its link to the winch line.

The brown-gray canvas undulated violently well above the heads of those below. It seemed to form an ominously large, pre-historic bird of prey flapping its dark wings. The force of the squall reached its peak. It tore the top of the tent from its connection to the ground and the unmoored beast rose high into the sky. The winds moved the flying canvas this way and that, and then, with the gale subsiding for a few moments, it

27

plummeted into the sea, not far from shore. The turbulently roiling waters caught it and began taking it further out.

"We've got to retrieve it!" Steerforth shouted above the wind, his pride injured by the failure of what, by then, he had taken to be chiefly his project. He immediately began a run to the beach. The others followed him to the shore, back to the same beached boat behind which Steerforth had earlier taken shelter. Still regarding himself as master and commander of the situation, Steerforth sought to right the boat, evidently considering using it to rescue the canvas from the ocean. There were two oars inside the boat. Steerforth picked one of them up to test its weight.

"You can't do it!" Copperfield shouted. "It's much too dangerous." Pip, equally alarmed by Steerforth's foolhardiness, turned to the only other man on the beach likely to be able to dissuade Steerforth from his recklessness. "Don't let him do it," he pleaded to Magwich. The former convict, not unaccustomed to violent confrontations, brought himself forward to Steerforth's side. He grabbed the oar from him. "It'll take two arms much stronger than your'n if it's to be done at all," he said, his height and bulk threateningly overpowering Steerforth's impulse to be the sole savior of the day. "No, Magwich," Pip cried out. "No! That's not what I meant. None of us should be so foolhardy." But Magwich was capable of a willful self-determination even steelier than Steerforth's. He ignored Pip's admonition and, demanding more than asking, adjured Steerforth to help him move the boat to the water. Chagrined, but grasping the implications of the situation, Steerforth complied.

It was clear to all there was no stopping Magwich. They joined in helping to move the boat. As soon as it had reached the water far enough to lift it, Magwich got in, placed both oars in their locks, and commanded a push farther into the sea. No one was certain how Magwich could manage to retrieve the canvas even if he got safely to it. The rush of events, however, impelled the others to follow his command. The perilousness of Magwich's solo endeavor, coupled with Steerforth's persisting pride, if not a sense of duty, and his willfulness, were no doubt what led Steerforth, to the horror of the others, to climb into the boat as it began its rise into deeper water.

# 8. The Boy and the Old Man Talk with Each Other About Youth and Old Age

Having circled the house to avoid the bustle in the kitchen and return most directly to the warmth of the fireplace, Scrooge entered the sitting room from the front door, the rising wind blowing at his back. Oliver remained seated where Copperfield had left him, still thinking about the men and women he knew to be present for the reception, and those Copperfield gave him reason to believe would not appear. His thoughts were purposed to see if he could discover what, if anything, united those present and divided them from the others.

Scrooge took the seat D.C. had vacated, smiling at both the warmth he anticipated by the fireside and the sight of the charming boy he had hosted with a cup of punch. The boy continued in his silent thoughts, leaving it to Scrooge to begin a conversation: "So, Oliver," he began with good cheer, "does the punch continue to warm you *within*?" Oliver broke his reverie to smile up at the old man. "Indeed, sir, you were quite right to foresee I wouldn't mind having a second cup." Twist's tactfully understated reply evoked a hearty laugh from Scrooge, and an encouragement. "Another will, I am sure, be served to you by and by," he responded. "But I observe that you seemed to be deep in thoughts when I came in, and perhaps have not yet abandoned them.

What deep thoughts might one so young as you be entertaining, I wonder."

"Well, not to be rude, sir, but among my thoughts was the question how it is that you—as well as myself—are here, and that some others that might be expected to come may not."

"As I saw from the first, young Oliver, you are a very clever boy.  I was myself, a very, very long time ago, also a clever boy. I have often reflected upon those days of my youth, and how things appeared to me then. I may have been a clever boy, but I was not—as sad to say as to remember—a happy one.  I trust you will not take offense if I ask you, Oliver: Do you think of yourself as a happy boy?"

"I have had my troubles too, Mr. Scrooge.  But the worst of them is over, I believe, and I hope that I would find myself as cheerful as you are if I was ever to grow up to be a man.  It would be easier then, I think, as it must have been for you, if I may say so."

"No, Oliver, my dear boy; I'm afraid that's not necessarily the case.  A man may have many troubles; devilish troubles of a kind a boy is not likely to have to bear.  That was so in my own case.  I assure you I was not always so cheerful as you see me today.  My prospects for some happiness have only recently improved.  Partly, I should tell you, because I am now blessed with the friendship of a boy even younger than you are, and of his family --to whom, I must confess, I was not formerly very cheerful."

The sound of the howling and whistling wind outside made itself heard within the sitting room as it crashed against the thin walls and windowpane of the Peggotty house.  The din and clatter might have disturbed the peace of the conversation, but Scrooge would not be displaced from his contentedness nor from his growing avuncular interest in his young companion at the fireside. "I should hope you will have a great many more happy memories by the time you are my age, Oliver."

"In point of fact, sir, you should know that I *am* about your age, and I shall never grow up to be a man, Mr. Scrooge. Mr. Dickens wouldn't let me. He seems to have liked me very much just as I am now."

"What an extraordinary thing you have just said, Oliver. I have no happy memories as a young boy and, from what you have said, neither you nor anyone else will know of any happy days you might have had as a grown man, let alone a very old one."

Oliver thought as deeply as he could about the significance of Scrooge's observation. It led him to wonder whether Scrooge's distressed and distressing thought might point toward solution of the mystery Copperfield had left with the boy to solve. "At least, Mr. Scrooge," he answered after his swift-minded reflections, "we can say that *right now and forever more*, waiting to see Mr. Dickens as we are, we are each happy."

Scrooge beamed. "I say, that is something, and a happy thought itself, I might add."

# 9. The Rescue of Two Characters, and Perhaps the Tent

"Wot ya be thinkin' uv, Mr. Steerforth?" Magwich shouted as the boat lifted over the first big wave it encountered, the oars propelled successfully to the task by his powerful arms. "You can't do it alone;" Steerforth replied above the din of the crashing water, "someone will have to haul the canvas. What were *you* thinking, Mr. Magwich?" As the oarsman continued a heroic struggle to get over the waves, fighting the wind as well as the water, he shouted back: "I thought to tie to a line from the canvas 'n bring it back close enough to shore to haul it in."

"You'll need another pair of hands to help, Magwich, I'm sure."

The four men on the beach witnessing the struggle of the little boat anxiously watched its slow progress. Pip and Copperfield, standing next to each other, could not conceal their distress. "If the wind keeps up," David said fearfully, "and a wave hits the wrong way, they could capsize." "Yes, I'm much afraid," Pip answered, "that the squall could be even too much for Magwich." "We can be thankful," David offered, encouraging some hope in himself as well as Pip, "they don't have too far to go."

"*They must be possessed!*" Grub cried out.

Carton, sharing the concern of all (but fortified by the large draughts of punch he had enjoyed) nevertheless remained composed. "We must prepare," he calmly advised, "to find some way to assist them, whatever may happen. Keep watch; I'll see what I can do." He left them on the beach and hurried back up to the house.

"Pray forgive my vehemence, ladies," Carton apologized as he burst through the kitchen door, "but the damn fools have gone off into the sea *in a rowboat* to rescue the tent!" *"Whhaaatt?!"* Betsey Trotwood exploded. Which damn fools?" "Steerforth and Magwich." Carton answered impatiently. "And where is Trot? My nephew David?," she anxiously inquired. "He's safe enough on the beach," Carton replied with even greater impatience. You needn't be concerned about him. The point is: does anyone know where there's a larger craft nearby to help if it's needed—as I've little doubt it will be."

"Oh, dear! Oh, dear!," Dora worried, in obvious agitation. Agnes tried to comfort her by reassuringly squeezing Dora's hand. "He said David is *fine*," she added to further allay her anxiety.

Peggotty came forward. "This is a fishing village, Mr. Carton," she explained. "There's lots of fishing boats docked up not far from here."

"Where would the nearest be? And who owns it?"

"Not an eighth of a mile away," Peggotty advised, "below the Bartles' house, just south of here."

By this time, Oliver and Scrooge, having heard the commotion following Carton's entry, had joined the others in the kitchen. Carton turned to Oliver. "Boy, get your coat on and run over to the Bartles' house south of here and tell Mr. Bartle what's happening. I'll follow right behind."

"I'll join you," Scrooge informed Carton with confidence, seizing an opportunity to assist. "I believe I may be able to be of some help, if need be. Mr. Bartle may require some compensation for the use of his boat."

"Oh, I doubt that," said Peggotty. "I'll come along with you to explain things to my neighbor."

"I think not, ma'am," replied Carton. "Best you stay here with the other ladies and continue with what you're doing. If we can manage to arrange things so they will turn out well, you'll still have a reception to attend to." Peggotty took Carton's admonition as the man's command, and made way for Carton and Scrooge to prepare to follow Oliver, who was already out the door.

Oliver had no trouble locating the Bartles' house, to which he'd sped as if with the footwings of Mercury. He quickly found Mr. Bartle and had swiftly sketched the outlines of the situation, which was about as much as he knew. But he had bad news for Carton and Scrooge by the time they arrived at the front door of the house to confirm the urgent need for help and negotiate the use of Bartle's fishing boat.

"His boat's in drydock, Mr. Scrooge," Oliver explained lamentably to his new friend. "Mr. Bartle says it would take more time to free it than will make it of any use. "

At the very moment this exchange was taking place, Magwich had got the boat within an oar's distance of the floating canvas. But it was still moving outward as its most well-soaked parts were struck by a strong undertow. Magwich maneuvered the boat round so Steerforth could reach for the canvas as soon as he could catch up with it. As he reached out to accomplish this crucial task, Steerforth leaned far over the stern

35

when a swell of the ocean hit the prow. The boat was turned over, violently casting both mariners into the water. Magwich grabbed on to the boat for dear life, not being much of a swimmer. The momentum of the boat's capsize had thrust Steerforth outward deep into the water, and he arose from it striking his head upon the underside of the canvas. In his struggle to clear himself from it, a line from the canvas wrapped around his right arm, and he had nearly exhausted his lung's supply of oxygen before he was able to return to the surface, attaining it some distance from the boat.

Copperfield, Pip, and Grub were still standing on the beach to monitor the boat's progress. By this time, though it was almost out of sight, they were able to see enough to grasp what was happening, and gasp at it. Seconds after they perceived the imminent disaster apt to follow from their friends' struggle in the water, at the height of their own distress, Grub began jumping up and down with excitement. "Lookeee, look there," he burst out, pointing to the east of the upturned boat's position. It was a fishing boat moving rapidly leeward toward the shore but within sight of the troubled duo. The fishermen on board spotted the pair and, disregarding their own peril, re-positioned the boat to make its way toward them. As they neared the capsized boat, they recognized the imminently fatal position Steerforth was suffering. He had already gone back down under the water twice, swallowing more of it than he could expel. The fishermen, shouting at him into the wind as loudly as they could make themselves heard, hastened their efforts to cast a line to him. Steerforth had just enough awareness left, and enough strength, to grab and hold on to it. He was very gradually hauled into the boat, falling prostrate, exhausted, onto its deck. "What about my friend? Is he safe?" he gasped from his prone position. "We're on the way to 'im," one of his rescuers replied.

Magwich's rescue was happily perfected. But, despite the man's ardent plea to the fishermen to make an effort to haul up the half-floating, half-sinking canvas from the water into their boat, the fishermen took another view of where the safety of all aboard lay, and resumed their effort to the shore, making their way to the Bartle's dock.

# 10. Two New Friends and Two Old Friends Have Needed Conversations

Magwich and Steerforth were returned to the Peggotty's house with the generous and kindly assistance of the fishermen, after they had successfully secured their boat. Steerforth remained barely conscious; he had to be half carried along the beach to the Peggottys. Upon his arrival there, Copperfield immediately led him into a bedroom, removed his boots and soaking clothes, and placed an old nightshirt of Mr. Peggotty's upon him. His strength not having yet returned, Steerforth was willingly laid in the one of the two beds usually occupied by Mr. Peggotty's son, Ham, little Emily's former betrothed. (The other bed belonged to the elder Peggotty. Neither of those two worthy Peggottys shall make an appearance in this story.) The half-drowned adventurer fell instantly into a deep sleep as soon as he felt the safety, warmth, and comfort of the bedclothes and pillows.

Copperfield returned to the sitting room to warm himself by the fire. There he found Magwich occupying the little rug in the center of the room, where he had placed himself when he was returned to the house with the support of the fishermen. A blanket had been thrown over him by Pip to add to his warmth. He was by this time propped upon pillows Pip had also provided for his greater comfort, drinking from a cup of heated punch Micawber had brought to him.

"I am highly gratified, Magwich, to see you returned here safely," Micawber had said as he delivered the hot drink to him. "Indeed, we all are. But I am loth to contemplate my own perplexities in considering whether I witnessed a courageous act or a foolhardy one in your effort to retrieve the canvas. Whatever impelled you, I wonder, to venture your very life—your very life I say—on such an extravagant undertaking as attempting to navigate a rowboat over the waves of an ocean turmoiled in a squall?"

Magwich quickly drained the cup and offered it to Pip. "Dear boy," he asked plaintively, "could ye kindly bring me another? I'm sure it will help take out more of the chill, just as the drink you gave me so many years ago did on that early Christmas mornin'." Pip immediately responded to his old benefactor's request, leaving Micawber alone with Magwich while he went to refill the cup. As soon as Pip had left the room, Magwich gave Micawber his answer: "I didn't want the boy to hear me say it, Micawber, for fear 'e would take too much upon hisself on it. I did it because *he* asked me to stop Steerforth, and I thought takin' the boat meself was the only sure way to do that, considerin' how that toff was thinkin'. Pip, the dear boy, helped me most kindly in an hour of great need, takin' risks he might have 'scaped takin'. How could I refuse 'im when I saw his great distress about his schoolboy chum, whatever I thought of the man meself, and me thinkin' I *could* do it?"

Micawber hesitated at first to respond to Magwich's noble reply to his question, but could not restrain himself from expressing an opinion. "I hope you won't take offense at my conveying my view of the matter but, in the spirit of candor, I must say I would have thought your time in Australia would have educated you to greater prudence in contemplation of manifest risks and your management of them."

This evoked a laugh from Magwich. "Ha, Micawber! If ye think goin' to Australia is the thing that has turned up to reverse your misfortunes, I can tell ya that it was only by takin' great risks that I managed to accum'alate the fortune allowin' me to help Pip grow up a gentleman!"

Copperfield had been a silent audience to this exchange, and he continued to sit in front of the fire after Pip and Micawber moved Magwich into the bedroom to help his recovery along more comfortably. After nearly an hour more had passed, Magwich having been well settled into deep sleep, Copperfield decided to look in again on Steerforth. He sat for a further long while beside him. Steerforth stirred, his eyes blinked awake, and he looked with mistaken gratitude up at Copperfield whom, in his lingering confusion, he momentarily inferred had been his rescuer. "Thank you," he murmured softly.

"Oh no, Steerforth," David corrected him; "it was not I who saved you or even brought you here. You and Magwich were rescued and brought here by a crew of fishermen. Do you know where you are, and in whose bed you lie?"

"Tell me, please."

"You are back at Peggotty's, and you are laying in Ham Peggotty's bed."

This news gave a shock to Steerforth. He raised himself up on the pillows and glanced around the room. "I'm not sure my wits have all returned, David, but since we are alone, now may be the time to talk about what you think happened. Oh, how I wish I could have changed it!"

"'*The moving finger writes,*'" David intoned with great dolor, "'*and, having writ, moves on: nor all thy piety nor wit shall lure it back to cancel half a line, nor all thy tears wash out a word of it.*'" And then he confessed sadly to his friend, "I realized too late for it to be of any use, that I did not rightly distinguish between what belonged to you that were gifts of nature, and what of your words and deeds expressed rather the cunning of art, acquired to help you achieve any willful end you chose."

"Don't be cruel, David. You must hear me out. I did abandon Emily, that is true. But you must not think it was wanton of me. I did love her, passionately, but she refused to be loved as a lady. She clung to her Yarmouth manners, and made it impossible for me to remain with her with any promise of true happiness for either of us. I tried to do all I reasonably could to secure a future for her with Littimer, with prospects not as high as I myself had sought for her to be sure, but closer to her own determined station in life. And, as for myself, my leaving her was the greatest effort I ever made to lead a worthy life. I chose to go to sea, not for mere adventure, but because it was where I believed I could challenge and test my mettle to better my poorly guided character. It was the noblest path I thought I could attempt, all things considered. Viewed in that light, was I so horribly wrong?"

"I would not question the goodness of your intentions, Steerforth; but your judgment was far from good and, to all the world—not least to Emily—had an appearance, not only of selfishness, but of the malign. And what you did exposed a flagrant want of your close attention to and regard for *her* sensibilities."

"I recognize, David, that is how it must have

41

appeared. Which is why I make this appeal to you, in all humility, for better understanding of my intentions and my motives. I am glad I am here, in fact, to put my case to Mr. Dickens, and to tell him he owes it to me to paint a fairer portrait; even, perhaps, to alter events to permit me not only to appear, but *to be* at my best to the very end."

"You know that will not be possible, Steerforth; the story is writ. Your own testimony and demeanor, indeed, your very plea, make it clear as day you know perfectly well that it had to turn out the way it did."

"Ah, David," Steerforth replied, with some condescension, "I would have thought you capable of a larger imagination. Mr. Dickens inhabits the country of the truly living. His capacities are far greater than yours or mine to direct matters as he may choose to direct them. I believe he, as our author, will be able to hear me out with a greater facility than you may possess—and greater means—to do justice to my character as, he will no doubt concede, he suggested it could be at its noblest."

Steerforth hastened to apologize for his lapse: "I beg your pardon, David, if it was arch of me to belittle your capacities. Will you at least suspend further judgment until Mr. Dickens and I have talked, and return yourself to the sentiments of the dear, dear old friend I know you to be?"

# 11. The Young Man and His Beloved Converse Before the Fire

Carton, Scrooge, and Oliver trudged their way, heads against the wind, down a hill toward the beach from which the rowboat had departed. Oliver, in an outburst similar to Grub's at the sight, alerted Carton and Scrooge to the fishing boat approaching the area in which they all rightly supposed the rowboat would by now have reached. They quickly conferred among themselves and, after considering the matter from several viewpoints, decided it likely they would make themselves most useful by returning to the Peggotty house, first, to inform the women that a rescue of Magwich and Steerforth from their predicament now seemed probable; and, second, to await the outcome in their company.

On their arrival, Scrooge and Oliver rushed into the kitchen to share the hopeful news, while Carton helped himself to another generous cup of punch and retired to enjoy the warmth of the fireside in the sitting room. But Carton was mistaken to believe he would thereby avoid the awkwardness of his uneasy society with persons of the opposite sex (whose company he only enjoyed with his one and only Manette), for he found Estella sitting there. There was no escaping the situation with grace, so, after making a courteous bow, he sat himself down before the fire in the chair across from hers.

Carton remained silent, either slowly sipping his cup of punch or contemplating it. Estella perceived his discomfort. She capriciously contrived to try to ease it. "You are Mr. Carton, I suppose," she guessed. "How do you suppose that?" Carton asked with surprise, turning his eyes from his cup to the lady. "I've learned a little about the guests who have so far arrived," she replied. "You're too old to be Oliver and too young to be Scrooge. I know that Magwich and Steerforth are out at sea. Pip is well known to me, and I have been given to understand that Copperfield is close to Pip's age, and that Mr. Carton is older than either of them. It's not a difficult inference."

"You are a detective, I see," rejoined Carton.

"But I really know so very little about you," Estella remarked ingratiatingly. "Would it be rude of me to ask you to tell me something about yourself?"

"There's nothing about my character of which I'd care to boast, dear lady; a jackal might more easily boast of his. And it's a gloomy thing to talk about one's past."

At this acerbic rejection, Estella was prepared to retreat. They were both saved from their mutual discomfort and further embarrassment, however, by Pip's entrance into the room. He greeted Estella in an obvious tone of ardent affection, giving an excuse for Carton to rise from his chair, offer his seat to Pip, and leave the room. Pip, accepting the offer with a smile, replied "I did not intend to displace you Mr. Carton, but thank you."

Now Pip and Estella were alone together, seated very near each other. The warmth of the fire helped to put each of them at ease as they sat silently for a few moments. It crackled with a fresh log that had been placed upon it, and its heat lent radiant fragrance to the perfume Estella was wearing. Leaning close to her, Pip was intoxicated by the scent; he closed his eyes in sensuous pleasure. He reached out for Estella's hand, hardly aware he was doing so. She allowed him the luxury of a touch, then slowly, with measured care, drew her hand away from his. He dreamily opened his eyes to gaze upon her. He was all surrender, and she was amused, as she so often had been when they were younger, by his captivation.

"Are you going to slap me again, Estella, as you did so many years ago, and try to make me cry?"

Estella smiled at this recollection of a scene from the very early days of their acquaintance. She reminded him that he had said then that she would never make him cry again.

"I have cried inwardly for you, and that is the sharpest crying of all. You must have seen how often you have made me cry for you that way. You must remember that I have continued to love you against reason, against promise, against peace, against hope, against happiness, against all discouragement that could be."

"And you must remember that I have no heart, if that has anything to do with my memory."

"But, in the end," Pip answered, drawing on his hopeful anticipation of a happy conclusion to their story, "Mr. Dickens will change our story as he first conceived it, to give you back your heart, so you may then return my love."

"He will have erred if he does that. Your love is too serious to become a trivially happy one. Its beginning was unhappy; its middle is unhappy; and for it to end happily would be an outrage. I would tell Mr. Dickens so if we speak to one another this evening."

She returned her hand to his, and allowed him to kiss it as she rose to leave. "I go to see how my father is doing, now that he's been rescued from the sea this time."

Despite what had almost become an habituation to such abandonments by Estella, Pip remained sitting by the fireside, softly weeping.

# **12.** Preparation for the Reception Resumes

It was the calm after the storm. The fiercely chilling winds, gradually subduing, had stopped. The Peggotty house was endowed with the first outer quiet of the day and the first promise of easier warmth. All those within became sensible to cessation of the wind outside. Its stilling paradoxically gave fresh breath to them, enabling them, each in his or her own way, to expel an outward or inward sigh of relief.

Copperfield had left Mr. Peggoty's room, leaving Steerforth in bed to continue his recovery. He went to the kitchen to see what was happening there. Upon his arrival he was immediately met with questions posed by his Aunt Betsey: "Well then, Trot, what shall we do now we have no tent? The house is already crowded nearly to its full. Where shall we put the other guests when they arrive?"

"I should not worry about that, Aunt Betsey," he assured her. "The storm will no doubt have discouraged most of them from coming, except for Mr. Dickens, of course. I'm sure he'll be resourceful at finding his way here, whatever the obstacles. And as to the others, when an author is aware of a predicament in which his characters are placed, and is sympathetic to their relief from it, he will certainly find a way to relieve them. I believe that Mr. Dickens, whose temperament I know almost as well as my own, shall be quite happy to be received only by those of us who have already arrived, and will be sure to manage that result. So, what

47

shall you do now? I speculate that Mr. Dick would advise us speedily to complete our preparations for Mr. Dickens' reception, for I predict he will soon arrive. It is nearly 6:00, and was he not expected at seven?"

"Ah, Trot, you and Mr. Dick set us all right! That is exactly what we should do. It appears to me that things may now turn out better than expected. We can see to it that our reception can be so arranged as to make the kitchen and the sitting room together compose an adequate arena for celebration of the arrival of our author. Indeed, will this not allow Mr. Dickens more commodious space enabling him to divide his attentions conveniently among us, at leisure, unencumbered by the press of too great a crowd in one place? Please let the others know at once that the reception *will* take place.

She shooed David out of the kitchen to make his appointed rounds and proceeded with despatch to manage with the help of Peggotty and Agnes final arrangements of the feast.

# 13. Charles Dickens Arrives and Is Questioned

The sound of his approaching carriage having alerted the household to Charles Dickens' imminent arrival, the question arose as to who should meet him at the door. Dora Copperfield instantly declined the honor, saying she had so many thoughts about it she didn't know *what* she would say to greet the author, beside which, she nervously explained, her aged dog, Jip, was ailing and required her attention. Miss Havisham would not think of it, nor would Estella. Aunt Betsey asked David for his opinion. DC suggested that a greeting by Agnes Wickfield would be most pleasing to CD, who had depicted her the very angel of femininity. (What man of feeling would not be pleased to be met by an angel at the door?) Even Peggotty who, as the resident of the house, would have seemed to be the logical choice, deferred to David's suggestion on the ground it would be "more proper."

All those present to receive their author were gathered round, Magwich and Micawber looking in from the kitchen portal and, within the sitting room, all the women seated and the men standing. Steerforth, having reassembled himself in his dried clothes, freshened with Peggotty's help, stood at the greatest distance. He was slouched against the wall opposite the fireplace, his hands in his pockets, the feet of his long legs nonchalantly crossed. He was set, however, to observe the proceedings closely.

The author arrived, happy to be met by Agnes at the doorstep, where she stood on her toes to reach his cheek with a kiss. He stepped inside, removed his hat, and paused to look around. His bright, sad, dark eyes surveyed the scene while a playful smile slightly curved his lips. The room was instantly transformed by his appearance; he dominated it from the moment he stepped inside from the threshold. Those awaiting his arrival, seeing him for the first time, regarded him with reverence; they were awed by his presence. Standing there in his greatcoat, with his ruffled bush of deep black hair and trimmed beard surrounding his intense gaze, an aura of magical powers seemed to radiate from Dickens' person. He appeared to all of them—even Steerforth—to be larger than life and the largest figure in the room—though in fact he was shorter than Scrooge, Magwich, or Steerforth. A complete stillness filled the sitting room for the few brief moments the author paused at the entry. As his hosts looked on to receive him, Dickens did not so much *sweep* into the sitting room as seem to *float* into it with easy steps, somehow raised above the floor.

Carton was the first to break the spell. He walked toward Dickens, tipsily took his hat, coat, and gloves; and led him to the most comfortable chair in the room—Mr. Peggotty's, not far from the fire. He offered to bring the author a cup of punch. The chilled and somewhat wearied traveler readily accepted. He made a gallant bow to Agnes, who had accompanied him to his chair, and then, upon seating himself, he again looked around the room. He addressed himself directly to the personage with whom he had the greatest rapport: "Well, David," he asked, "kindly enlighten me: what is the plan for the evening, and what is expected of me?"

"We shall have a feast, Mr. Dickens, which the ladies have spent the day preparing. But first, as soon as you can let us know you are sufficiently refreshed to help entertain the company, there are those among us who have questions they wish to ask you."

Carton was quick to bring Dickens a large cup of punch, which the guest of honor gratefully took in hand. "I believe," said Dickens in response to Copperfield's advisement, "that the contents of this cup, and satisfaction of my curiosity about the questions that will be asked of me, will together be likely to refresh me sufficiently to permit us to begin without delay." He took a deep draught of the punch. "Who wishes to be the first to question me?" There was a short interlude of silence, and then, "Oliver!" Dickens exclaimed with pleasure, as he saw the boy come over to him and offer a deep, courteous bow. "Oliver, my boy, how do you do?"

"I'm very fine now, thank you sir," Twist answered in the best of cheer.

"And what question do you have for me?"

"More than one, Mr. Dickens. Since Mr. Copperfield has hinted that you are responsible for choosing those to be present at your reception, could you please tell me why you admitted some and refused others of your characters to be here?"

Dickens was evidently pleased by the question. "You might have noticed, dear boy, that there has been excluded from this assembly all the *unqualified villains* to be found in my writings, and also the saddest victims of their perfidy. As to the former, who would willingly seek their company? (Although I would rather have liked to see Uriah Heep here, with Mr. Micawber confronting him once again and putting him in the truly

51

humble—that is to say, *humiliated*—place he deserved.) And as to the latter, my heart would burst apart and I would drown myself in my own tears were I to find myself in the midst, at once, of those who were made to suffer the most aggravated injuries. I do not have a heart of stone, and could not laugh at the death of Little Nell. No, for the comfort of *my* character, I should admit only those for whom I cherish some affection or admiration and whose misfortunes, considering my part in bringing them about, are more or less bearable—that is, not strictly intolerable—to their tender-hearted author. And, as to those of you who are present, I have chosen for you to appear at the most vivid stages of your being, while keeping you conscious of the ends you each shall achieve.

"Finally, as to the limit in the number admitted overall, the circumstances of our location and the modest space available to accommodate us without discomfort—or tedium to our readers—have been my guides."

After considering Dickens' reply to his question for a moment or two, Oliver posed his more perplexing question. "And how can it be, Mr. Dickens that you, if you'll pardon my asking, having passed on to your mortality, are here among us?"

"That, Mr. Oliver Twist, to borrow a countryman's elegant construction in paraphrase, 'is a riddle, wrapped in an enigma, inside a mystery' that will be unwrapped to all and its solution disclosed by the end of this very story in which we find ourselves at the present time. The answer to your question would, I believe, best await my answers to questions others may have."

Estella had also taken a seat close to the fireplace, not far from where Dickens sat. "I have a far different kind of question, Mr. Dickens."

"Please Estella, I'd like to hear it."

"That remains to be seen, sir," she coldly replied. "I suggest, Mr. Dickens, with all warranted respect, that it was nothing other than a want of fortitude, and I might say, commitment to the verity of things, that led you to rewrite Pip's story and mine to please your readers with an artificially happy conclusion to what, in truth, must have ended sadly. Can you deny that in my presence?"

"Or have the impertinence to deny it in mine?" added Miss Havisham.

The author was understandably taken aback by this onslaught upon his integrity as a writer by two of the beings he had created, although he was, of course, quite aware of the misanthropy of which the two women just questioning him were each capable. "May I defend myself," he asked, "by pointing to the high unlikelihood that even a character such as yourself, Estella, could forever remain invulnerable to a love as pure as Pip's, a young man as handsome, as fortunate, and as generally amiable as Pip was drawn to be?"

"You rightly say, sir, as *generally* amiable. In fact, he had become much of a snob, and his senseless ardor was always unattractive to me. If verisimilitude had been your guide, we never would have married. It is an outrage that you re-contrived our story to conclude with such an unlikely romance." And she added, with chilly vehemence: "I dare say that your own reputation has become such that your error should not be irremediable and may be corrected."

53

Dickens was embarrassed at this indictment which, in fact, he had suffered from the spoken and written words of others. He was preparing to augment his defense by recitation of the legitimate worldly concerns of an author dependent upon the good will and enthusiasm of his readers, when David interjected, thinking to spare him Estella's further proud cruelties. "There is quite an opposite question at hand, Mr. Dickens. It is one in which I have a great interest, although it is not my own." He looked toward Steerforth. "Come Steerforth, is it not now the time to air your grievance?"

Steerforth took his hands out of his pockets, uncrossed his legs, and altered his casual posture against the wall from a slouching to an erect position. He walked slowly across the small room with short, deliberate steps to where Dickens was sitting and Copperfield stood beside him. He directed his response to the latter. "In my view, David, what I have to say and to ask pertain to a supremely personal matter, not fit for airing to those not concerned, and potentially disturbing, if not offensive, to those who are. I would prefer, indeed I would insist, to have my conversation with Mr. Dickens in private, if he would condescend to consider what I have said already, and grant me a personal audience." He turned toward Dickens, looking him in the eyes with the pregnant silent question his words manifestly implied.

Dickens looked up to David inquisitively, and saw in *his* eyes an earnest plea to grant his old friend's request. "Where, Mr. Steerforth," the author asked in an even tone after a pause, looking toward his intimate inquisitor, "would you prefer to have this private conversation take place?" Steerforth gestured toward

54

Mr. Peggotty's bedroom. Dickens rose, and preceded Steerforth into the indicated room of his choice.

Dickens took a few steps into the bedroom and turned toward Steerforth, who had entered immediately behind him. They remained standing facing each other after Steerforth had closed the portal curtain to assure their privacy. The author invited their conversation. "Well, Mr. Steerforth, what have you got to say to me—and ask?"

"I believe, Mr. Dickens, you will readily anticipate the gist of my complaint. It is, as you might well have guessed, that in your purpose to startle your readers with a shocking melodrama, you did me a grievous injustice. You cast aside all those qualities which, in their expression, made me a hero to my loyal friend, David, and captivated your audience. You turned the imperfections of my character, attributable to my mother's loving indulgences, into absolute *vice*, giving me the appearance, in the end, of a wanton, wicked villain. I put it to you, Mr. Dickens, that you need not have treated me so malevolently; that envy of my higher station in life than your own impelled you to bring me down; and that you could have and should have put a more accurate and sympathetic—not to say *charitable*—face on the circumstances that led to my elopment (as it were) with Emily, and to my abandonment of our liaison as the result of a patent *necessity*. I therefore ask you, as Estella did, to correct this injustice in the opposite direction of the one you did to her and Pip; that is, to recraft your story with a happier and more fitting version of events, considering the great hopes and expectations you had raised for me with your readers."

Dickens looked upon him sternly. He was not timid in his reply: "Your capacity, Mr. Steerforth, for selfishness, cruelty, and wantoness were illustrated from the outset of your appearance. You charmingly bilked David of his meager means; were shown to have done wicked injury as a child to the young Miss Dartle, who loved you, with a hammer to her face, forever disfiguring her. And your contempt for those who suffered a lower station in life than the one you enjoyed—with the exception of David—was repeatedly demonstrated. You are, in fact, Mr. Steerforth, a determined snob. You were given every indulgence and comfort—indeed, luxury—a privileged young man could hope to enjoy. You were equipped by both nature and art to display an irresistible charm to those you wished to ingratiate. But all that was nothing in comparison to the ease with which you embraced your willful and wicked impulses. I owe you no apology."

Steerforth moved in closer to Dickens. "You overstate your case, Mr. Dickens, I am sure. Did you not make—and find—me very attractive from the first?" He moved even closer, placing his left hand on Dickens' shoulder and looked him straight in the eye. "I was very grateful to you for making me so," Steerforth breathed to him, softly. "Did you yourself not find me very interesting?" Steerforth allowed his hand to move along Dickens' shoulder, so close upon his neck that its radiant youthful warmth was felt. He smiled at the author, exuding the almost hypnotic charm of which both knew he was capable. "I mean," he paused, "really *interesting*? Just as I said it would be interesting to meet Daisy's sister, if he had one?" Dickens, nearly placed under Steerforth's spell, resisted an impulse, quite foreign to him in most circumstances, to return the warm touch of Steerforth's hand, now directly upon his neck, with an embrace. Instead, he leaned forward to whisper in Steerforth's ear: "You cannot touch or change or injure *me*, sir. Nor can you seduce me to alter what I have done and who I am. I have become as unalterable as you and all the others. I have become –to answer Oliver's question about the mystery of my appearance among you—I have become—*a character.* And it would not be a misplaced wish for me to say with Tiny Tim, *'God bless us, every one!'* Even you, Mr. Steerforth, of whom I will always wish to think at your best.

"Now let us return to the sitting room, where we both belong, so we may enlighten not only Oliver, but all with the truth in the being of my appearance."

# 14. Two New Lovers Meet

Steerforth had been humiliated. He stood alone quietly in the bedroom for a few moments after Dickens had left to return to the reception. His feelings vacillated between anger at the world without, the world within which his character had been fixed, and with himself. *"Neither master of another, nor master of myself!"* he raged inwardly. He walked about the little room, seething. There was one small straight-backed wooden chair in the corner. He picked it up and crashed its legs against the floor repeatedly, wanting to destroy it, to disintegrate it, absolutely to crush it into the nothingness for which he himself at that moment longed. His rampant rage exhausted, he sat down on Ham Peggotty's bed, then lay back upon it. He closed his eyes hoping, for a passing instant, to obtain that oblivion of which sleep's brief hours give us a taste. But he recognized, almost immediately, that sleep would be impossible. Raising himself up from his prone position, he heard voices coming from the sitting room, to which Dickens had returned. He knew he was obliged to join the on-going reception, but knew with greater certainty that he could not do that, at least not yet.

The alternative he took was quietly to leave the bedroom, escape to the kitchen without being noticed, and exit the rear of the house to the grounds where the lost canvas had been laying that morning.

The night air was extremely chill, but the wind had stilled and the cold was bearable. In fact, it seemed to him to echo the refrigerating cold that had descended upon himself. The moon was full, casting its pale ghostly light upon the earth. Entering that light, Steerforth thought of himself as a ghost, the substance of his being emptied, bereft of pride, arrogance, and even will. Then he heard a woman's voice, speaking to someone else. He looked in the direction of the couple, standing close to one another just a few feet away. It was Magwich and Estella, father and daughter, who, meeting one another that day, had left the reception and ventured outside the house to speak to each other for the first time, in private. Steerforth's noticed arrival nearby interrupted the intimacy of their conversation.

An aura of cold enchantment within the ghostly light surrounded the trio. It froze all three of them into a magical tableau as Magwich and Estella gazed toward Steerforth and Steerforth gazed back at them. Estella was wearing a white satin cloak. It shined in the moonlight and illuminated her features so sharply Steerforth could see them clearly. He was spellbound by what he saw. An uncanny electricity passed between the young man and woman, sustaining their frozen postures and reciprocal regard for a few further moments.

Magwich, whose imperfect vision had to adjust to recognize Steerforth, broke the silence and the spell. "Mr. Steerforth," he explained, thinking an explanation was needed, "this be me daughter, Estella." The old man turned his face back to Estella's. "Estella, this be Mr. Steerforth, the man who tried to help me in the boat." Steerforth moved closer to the couple. Despite his inward devastation, the impact Estella had made upon him revived his gallantry. "It is a great pleasure, my lady," he said with a courtly bow. Estella, as intrigued by Steerforth as he had been with her, offered her hand to permit him to kiss it. He did so with gratitude and grace, looking up into her eyes with a fervor she could not miss. "I have more to ask you," she said to Magwich, "but I think it best we should now return inside." There was no doubt in Estella's mind that her wish would be a command to Magwich so, correctly presuming her father's consent, she addressed Steerforth: "Will you join us, Mr. Steerforth?" she inquired, equally certain of the result. Magwich, attempting the part of a gentleman, stood aside and allowed Steerforth to accompany his daughter back into the warmth of the Peggotty's kitchen.

Estella's *sang-froid* had been the product of Miss Havisham's careful breeding. Steerforth's breeding, amplified by his charm, endowed him with an hauteur that gave the two of them the outward appearance of kindred types, though the sources of their characters were, in reality, quite different. But the result was, in both cases, an extraordinary magnetism which, on that night, drew them to each other with the intensity of a kind neither had felt before in the presence of anyone else. The Peggotty's kitchen was not a setting appropriate for any sort of expression of the unique feelings each, unexpectedly, was feeling for the other. They wordlessly recognized, however, the bond that had instantly been formed between them. It was, therefore, with complete understanding that Estella, her *sang-froid* broken, silently acknowledged with agreement Steerforth's quietly saying to her as they entered the kitchen, "We shall, I presume Estella, see more of each other in future."

It would, as we know, have to be so in another life.

## 15. The Eldest Congregate and Consider Their Regard for Mr. Dickens

The four gathered in the kitchen awaiting Mr. Dickens' return from his private conversation with Steerforth were, perhaps, the most striking intimate assembly of that day's events, for at least two reasons. First, each had lived (and one had died) in a different one of Dickens' writings. Second, the group constituted the eldest congregation of four that could be collected among the guests. To be particular, it consisted of Betsey Trotwood, Miss Havisham, Ebenezer Scrooge, and Gabriel Grub. Their combined years substantially exceeded the number of those lapsing from the date of Mr. Dickens' birth to its 200th anniversary.

After some congenial trivialities exchanged among them over the bowl of punch, Betsey Trotwood began a more serious conversation by inquiring of Miss Havisham: "And what, pray let us know, Miss Havisham, might you complain of to our author concerning his treatment of you?"

Miss Havisham was horrified. "Why," she replied, "were I to begin to complain there would be nothing left of me by the time my complaints ended! There isn't *anything* he gave to me in which I might rejoice! The origin of the condition in which Pip first found me was not only a scandal and an embarrassment, it was a disgrace. The circumstances in which I was consistently found in the sequel were nothing other than hideous to one of ordinary sensibilities. Moreover, the portrait he drew of me throughout was one of a determined and irremediable misanthropy, promoting the absolute torture of any man over whom I might exert some control through Estella. And, finally, the termination of my existence provided for by his art was an unbearable agony demonstrating a lack, I have always supposed, of even a shred of pity for me. No, I shall have to remain silent, or I will disappear altogether."

Scrooge towered over the diminutive Miss Havisham. He was at first stunned by her outburst. But as he observed the increasing ardor of her rage at Trotwood's question, he began to take pity on her, and looked at her from above with an expression of such intense empathy it could not even escape Miss Havisham's notice. He had an impulse to take her hand in his as a small comfort, but he knew she would find that insupportable and reject it with indignation as an affront. "My dear lady," he managed to eke out after she concluded, "my dear, dear lady. You must think of the matter differently, I am sure. I can tell you, from my own experience, that repentance is never too late if only it comes while there still is life. If you could have but put aside and repented your chronic melancholy, if you could have but retrieved yourself from the bitterness whose awful taste and effect was keenest in your own mouth and heart, you might have found a way to displace the love and loss of your intended betrothed with love for the poor, beautiful child you took in, and let your heart heal by helping to grow hers into that of a loving young woman. We are capable, I assure you, of such changes if we only are given the will, which Mr. Dickens may have been able to provide you."

"Ha!" returned Miss Havisham, with curled lips.. "Ha, Humbug! If what you have said is a teaching you learned from Mr. Dickens, you were tutored by hypocrisy and cant. You heard of the outrage he practiced upon Estella and Pip—and thereby upon myself. A proper regard for the likelihood of things should have halted his hand to pretend a happy ending to their story. There are sufferings of those who appear fortunate that can far exceed the ordinary suffering of those in want, whose main complaint is the lack of an easy sustenance. There are wounds to the heart that may cause a far more severe and lasting pain even than an empty stomach, which is easily satisfied by morsels. Don't speak to me of a 'repentance' that could not have been."

Now it was Scrooge who was appalled. But he would not be daunted. "Please, Miss Havisham," he pleaded, "please join with me for another cup of this punch you so kindly helped to provide for us, and collect yourself to consider further what I have said."

"I can tell ye, Miss Havisham, that wot he says ain't a lie," added Grub. "It may take a shock, but a hardened heart can be softened. The goblins shud've got ya and done ya the kind of good they did me."

"Fantasy, Mr. Grub," she replied, "sheer fantasy!"

"Calm yourself, Miss Havisham! Calm yourself, I say!" exclaimed Aunt Betsey. "I was never married, and that did no ill to *my* heart. Not at all. I should have been much less happy had I been obliged to be a helpless servant denominated a 'wife' by most of the men I have encountered—in a life nearly as long as your own."

"Indeed, Miss Trotwood," said Mr. Charles Dickens, who had been listening at the kitchen door since the latter part of Miss Havisham's first outburst.

"And that is the kind of character you possess and the character you are. The fact that you suffered no hardened heart from your want of matrimony was evident in the loving charity and care you demonstrated for your nephew David, of whom I am as fond as you are." He turned his attention to Miss Havisham.

"I assure you, my dear woman, that there was no want of pity in me for your condition, nor want of caring about your plight. I wept for you on many a page as it was being written, and only very reluctantly brought you to the end I thought fated by what had preceded it. You were not without some responsibility, you must confess, in causing that awful fate by the fireplace to be realized." Miss Havisham was nonplussed by these remarks. She looked upon Mr. Dickens with wonder, and with newly respectful admiration. *"You cared about me?"* she asked.

"Of course I did, Miss Havisham. I have cared deeply about all my characters. My special care for you was most demonstrated, don't you see, in the unique poignancy of the personality you exhibit among all the characters in my writings. How could any reader doubt the existence in you of an exquisite sensibility reflecting a tender and loving heart, seeing it was one that could be so deeply and thoroughly broken?"

*"Really*, Mr. Dickens? Do you really think so? 'Tender and loving?'"

"Most certainly."

He was bolder than Scrooge and, moving close to her, gently took her hand in his. He spoke softly to her, barely above a whisper: "Come. Miss Havisham, let us fetch your coat and cloak. The wind has stopped, and the sight of the ocean from Yarmouth beach, rolling and shining beneath tonight's full moon, is made to be

64

viewed with pleasure by both youthful and aged lovers." She started at his reference to lovers, but he went on. "The mysterious beauty so near to us will make us forget the cold night air. Such a sight, savored in the company of a caring friend, redolent of the mysterious charm only the natural world can radiate, is likely to stir a heart such as yours with tenderness, as it stirs my own." He took her other hand in his  "It would be the greatest pleasure for me to take you there—just you and I—so we may quietly enjoy it together, and listen to the watery heartbeat of the world, and let our own hearts beat as one with it."

She had no words to say in reply, and permitted him to lead her to the closet where her coat and cloak hung. Taken thoroughly out of herself by Dickens' words, and mesmerized by recognition of a manly affection for herself which, she now recognized, had abided throughout her existence, she meekly accepted his invitation.

And they lived happily ever after, don't you know?

# AFTERWORD & LITERARY NOTES

*"We meet on this day to celebrate the birthday of a vast army of living men and women who will live for ever with an actuality greater than that of the men and women whose external forms we see around us."*
—**Charles Dickens**, at the Garrick Club, April 22, 1854, on the celebration of Shakespeare's birthday.

It may be surprising to some to consider how Charles Dickens' characters have so widely and deeply penetrated our culture. Through their adaptation over the past century to stage, screen, television and, most recently, even YouTube, they have becomes icons of mass culture. Even many of those who have never read a line of Dickens can recognize and have associations with a good many of them. One does not have to be well-educated to have some idea of who Ebenezer Scrooge is, and what his name signifies. (Think of Scrooge McDuck.) Even aficionados of popular culture may more likely have heard of Dickens' Tiny Tim and his Christmas blessing than the comic entertainment figure of the last century who went by the same name. The name of Bob Cratchit, and those of Oliver Twist and Fagin; Wilkins Micawber and Uriah Heep; Pip, Estella and Miss Havisham, and Mr. Pickwick are also among those whose fictional personas have translated into recognized types. These and other Dickensian creations embody qualities we admire or detest; feel empathy or pity for; laugh at, or rejoice or sorrow with.

Dickens' characters are so recognizable to us partly because he created many of them with the vividness and vivacity of technicolor cartoons, in a kind of fabulist fiction that suspends our disbelief at their larger-than-life (or smaller-than-life) improbability. Indeed, Dickens has been criticized for creating cartoons and lampoons rather than realistic characters, and for contriving scenarios so outlandish that, even when their purpose is to affect us with horror or sorrow, they cannot be taken seriously. It was with this viewpoint in mind that Oscar Wilde famously said "One must have a heart of stone to read the death of Little Nell without laughing." But Dickens has given us many of his characters in more than two dimensions; he invites us to see some of them in the round. Their being may echo in our minds in a variety of ways: Scrooge, the miser; Scrooge, the redeemed; Scrooge, the suffering child and the unloving lover; Scrooge, Tiny Tim's savior. Pip, the frightened, innocent boy; Pip, with great expectations; Pip, the perenially hopeless lover; Pip, the unlikely snob. And, one of his most intriguingly layered characters, Steerforth, the heroic champion of his schoolmates; Steerforth the charmer; and Steerforth the licentious villain.

The poet Percy Shelley told us that "Poets are statesmen." By that I think he meant that our true *cultural and ethical* constitutions are formed by what our poets (in the largest sense of that word) give us, and how their creations affect our consciousness and attitudes. It is, therefore, not only an academic question to consider our psycho-logical reactions to and interactions with fictional characters who have become embedded in our consciousness, implanted icons of good and bad behavior. Some of them may indeed live with us *"ever with an actuality greater than that of the men and women whose external forms we see around us."*

The story told in *A Visitation By Charles Dickens* accordingly transgresses the border between the fictional and the factual and defies the strictures of time and narrative logic. Its characters are depicted thriving at some period before their stories have ended but are nevertheless fully aware of what those endings will be—that is, have already been. And why shouldn't they be depicted as so aware? Pip says, in retrospectively recounting the story of his feelings for Estella in *Great Expectations*, "I know what I know of the pain she cost me afterwards."

In *A Visitation*, Dickens' characters have escaped the bounds imposed upon them by their author; and they have some issues with him. (This conceit is partly inspired by Luigi Pirandello's play, *Six Characters in Search of An Author*.) The mini-dramas of the story reflect, in one way and another, the central dramas of the novels in which the characters appear. Steerforth and Magwich, for example, in *David Copperfield* and *Great Expectations*, respectively, both die in the sea, as they are threatened with death in *A Visitation*. Pip, as in *Great Expectations*, looks at his love for the girl who declares herself to be without a heart from a very different perspective than the girl's. But the story also permits some of the characters to boil over from their assigned fates in the novels and try to tempt Dickens to reconsider their endings. It is a fact that Dickens wrote two versions of the ending of *Great Expectations*, exactly as Estella accuses him of doing in *A Visitation*. In her indictment of Dickens, Estella is paraphrasing George Bernard Shaw, who wrote that *Great Expectations* "is too serious a book to be a trivially happy one. Its beginning is unhappy; its middle is unhappy; and the conventional happy ending is an outrage on it." What might Pip and Estella say to each other as well as to Dickens with foreknowledge of that fact?

And what would Steerforth, liberated from the confines of his depiction in the novel *David Copperfield*, say to his author?

Might we not also entertain some curiosity, for further examples, about how Scrooge, after his redemption, would behave in the world outside of Christmas? Or how Pip and Steerforth, Steerforth and Sydney Carton, Steerforth and Estella, or Magwich and Micawber, might relate to one another if they met? What would Betsey Trotwood say to Miss Havisham, and how would she react to Havisham's intractable morbidity? The story makes suggestions to satisfy such curiosity and related questions we might ask from our encounters with Dickensian characters, including particularly how his characters might react to *him*..

Finally, *A Visitation By Charles Dickens* suggests that what we can learn and know of people who have actually walked the earth may be no more—and probably even less—than what we can learn and know about the characters novelists as great as Dickens have created. It also suggests that we may be able to go beyond a novelist's depiction of his characters to conceive potential attributes the novelist might have been reluctant or unwilling to expose, dimensions of their being we are free to *infer* from what Dickens has given us. It was famously said that "History is bunk." I wonder whether whoever said that therefore thought that some fiction may not be. It is a very ancient opinion that poetry is a greater literary form than history.

**July 4, 2012**

Made in the USA
Charleston, SC
09 December 2012